AF580939

ANDROMEDA

The Myth and Science of Astronomy

Simon Rose

Go to **www.openlightbox.com**, and enter this book's unique code.

ACCESS CODE

LBG38865

Lightbox is an all-inclusive digital solution for the teaching and learning of curriculum topics in an original, groundbreaking way. Lightbox is based on National Curriculum Standards.

STANDARD FEATURES OF LIGHTBOX

AUDIO High-quality narration using text-to-speech system

ACTIVITIES Printable PDFs that can be emailed and graded

SLIDESHOWS Pictorial overviews of key concepts

VIDEOS Embedded high-definition video clips

WEBLINKS Curated links to external, child-safe resources

TRANSPARENCIES Step-by-step layering of maps, diagrams, charts, and timelines

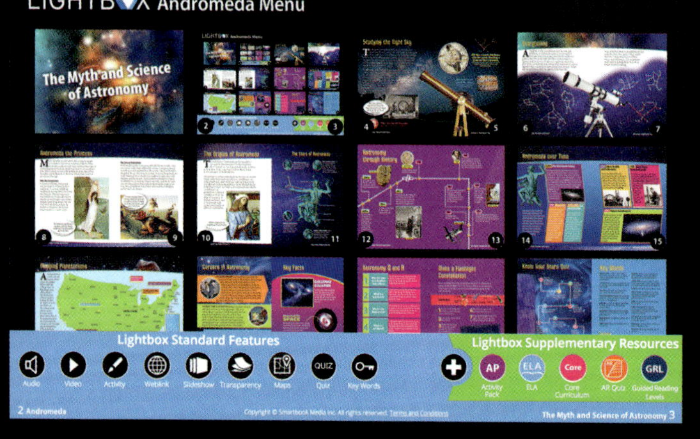

INTERACTIVE MAPS Interactive maps and aerial satellite imagery

QUIZZES Ten multiple choice questions that are automatically graded and emailed for teacher assessment

KEY WORDS Matching key concepts to their definitions

Contents

Studying the Night Sky

The study of stars and other objects in space is called astronomy. Groups of stars that form patterns in the night sky are known as constellations. They appear in different parts of the sky at different times of year. There are also some constellations that can be seen only from the Northern or the Southern **Hemisphere**. A star chart, or map of the sky, helps sky watchers find constellations.

Civilizations in the Middle East began naming stars and constellations thousands of years ago. About the same time, people named the signs of the zodiac. The zodiac is an imaginary band in the sky divided into 12 constellations that represent characters and animals. The first **telescopes** were used to study the stars in the early 17th century. Today, scientists called astronomers use large, powerful telescopes to observe **comets**, **galaxies**, stars, and planets. Planets are large objects in space that travel around a star, such as Earth or Mars moving around the Sun.

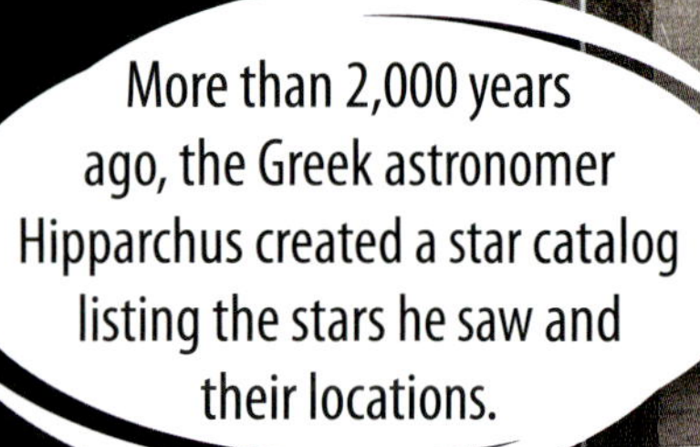

The ancient Greeks described many of the constellations.

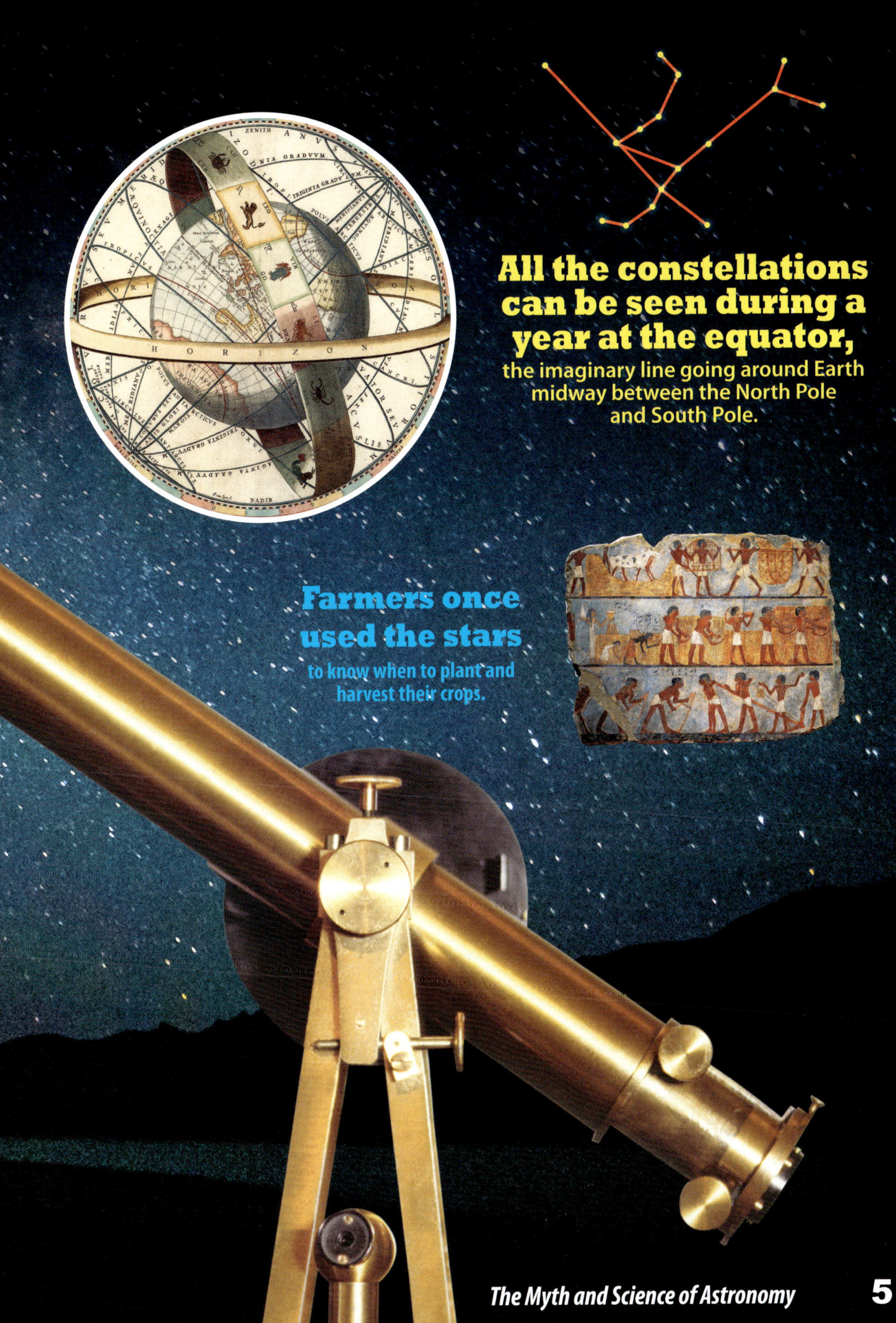

All the constellations can be seen during a year at the equator,

the imaginary line going around Earth midway between the North Pole and South Pole.

Farmers once used the stars

to know when to plant and harvest their crops.

Storytelling

Around the world, constellations have become part of folklore, or traditional customs, stories, and art. Throughout history, people have tried to explain the patterns they saw in the night sky. They created imaginary figures using the stars in the sky, as in a game of connect the dots. Some constellations were named after characters in ancient legends. Other constellations were named after animals. People also created stories about the figures in the night sky.

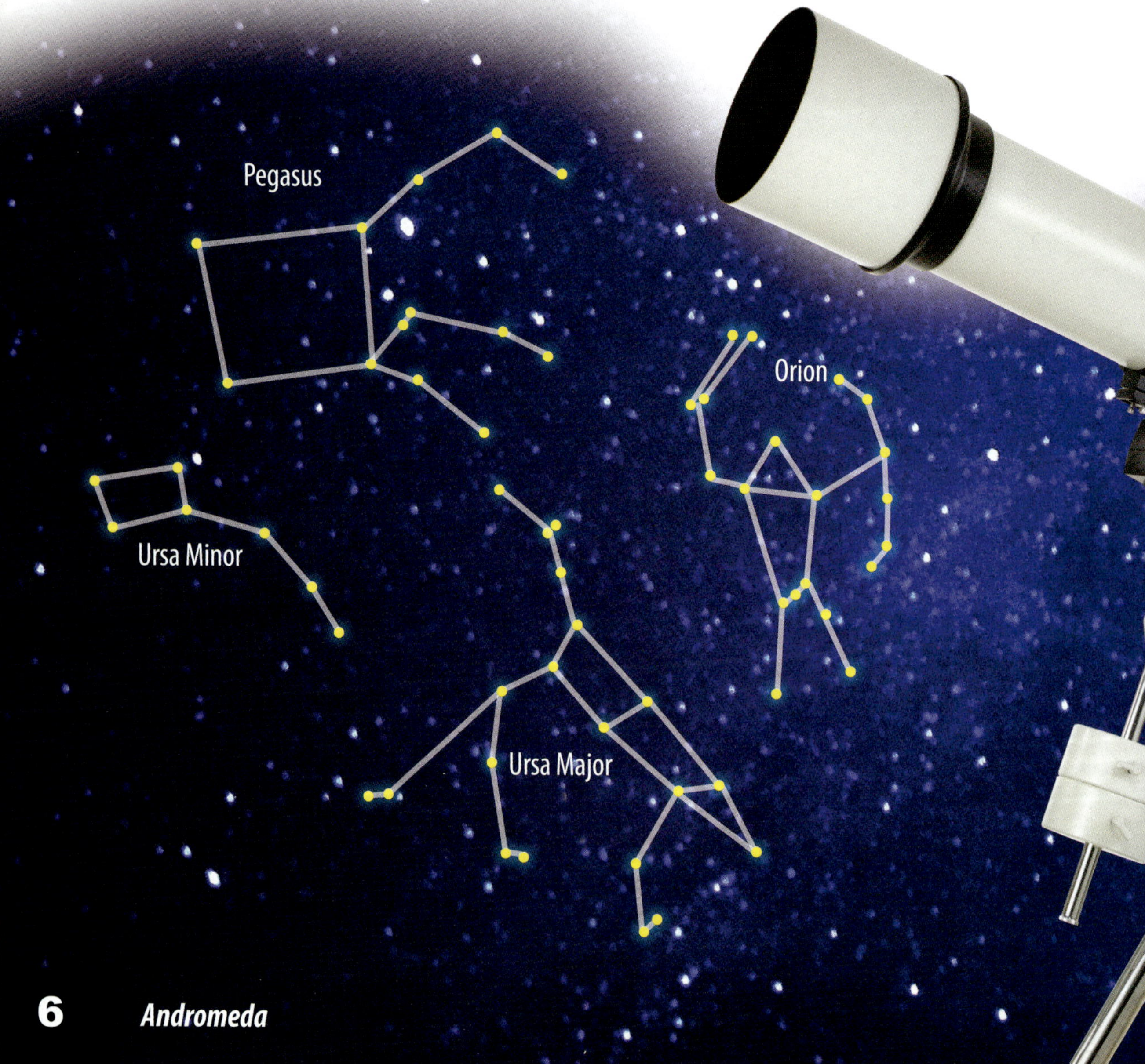

Some of the best-known constellations are seen in the Northern Hemisphere. They include Hercules, Cygnus, Pegasus, Ursa Major, Orion, and Andromeda. The constellation Andromeda is named after a character in ancient Greek storytelling.

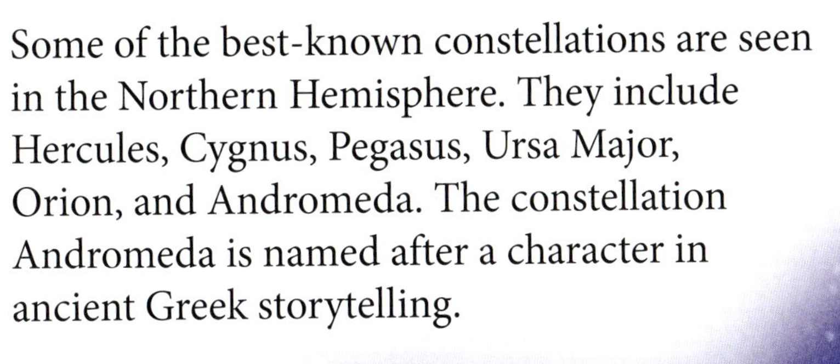

Andromeda the Princess

Many constellations are named after imaginary people or creatures in the stories of different cultures. These stories are usually very old. Some are about the origin of a cultural group and how the people first came to live in a certain area. Others explain events in the world such as thunderstorms, droughts, and earthquakes. Collections of these types of stories are called mythology.

Who Was Andromeda?

In Greek mythology, Andromeda was the daughter of King Cepheus and Queen Cassiopeia of Ethiopia. Andromeda was married to the Greek hero Perseus. They had many sons. One of them was Perses, who was an ancestor of the Persians. One of their daughters was Gorgophone. She was married to two kings and was the mother of Tyndareus. He became king of Sparta in ancient Greece.

The Andromeda constellation is sometimes called "the chained maiden" after one of the legends about Andromeda.

The Story of Andromeda

Andromeda's mother, Cassiopeia, offended the sea nymphs. They were spirits in the shape of beautiful women. Cassiopeia claimed that she was more beautiful than the nymphs. They told Poseidon, the god of the sea. He sent a sea monster to destroy King Cepheus's lands. The king had to sacrifice his daughter to make peace with Poseidon and the nymphs. Andromeda was chained to a rock to be killed by the sea monster. Perseus saved her, and the two were married. The goddess Athena placed Andromeda's image in the stars. Her constellation is near those of her mother, Cassiopeia, and her husband, Perseus.

The Origins of Andromeda

The constellation Andromeda was first included in star maps by the astronomer Claudius Ptolemy in the 2nd century AD. The story of Andromeda, however, is much older. It may come from myths in Mesopotamia, an ancient region in the Middle East.

Astronomers in various lands placed the stars that the ancient Greeks called Andromeda into different constellations. An Arab constellation called al-Hut was made up of stars in the constellations Andromeda and Pisces. In the Marshall Islands in the Pacific Ocean, stars from Andromeda and other nearby constellations are grouped into a different constellation. It has the shape of a porpoise. In Chinese astronomy, stars in Andromeda make up parts of a number of different constellations.

Ptolemy studied math and geography as well as astronomy.

The Stars of Andromeda

Alpha Andromedae This is the brightest star in the constellation. It forms Andromeda's head. It is also called Alpheratz or Sirrah.

Beta Andromedae This star is the second-brightest in the constellation. It is also called Mirach. That name comes from the Arabic word *mizar*, meaning "girdle." Beta Andromedae is a type of star known as a **red giant**.

Alpha Andromedae

Beta Andromedae

Upsilon Andromedae

Gamma Andromedae

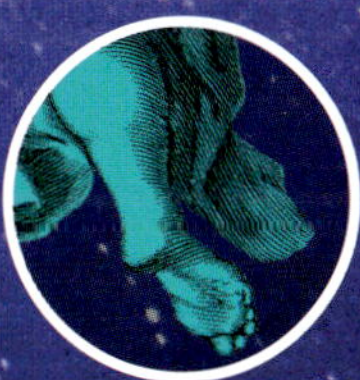

Gamma Andromedae
The third-brightest star is also called Alamak or Almach. It appears to be a single star, but it is really a star system made up of four stars of different colors.

Upsilon Andromedae Upsilon Andromedae is a pair of stars known as a **binary star** system. Four planets **orbit** the main star. Astronomers believe that these are **gas giant** planets similar to Jupiter.

Astronomy through History

3000 BC

The Sumerians, in the Middle East region known as Mesopotamia, make lists of the brightest stars and name the constellations in the zodiac for the first time.

2500 BC

In Mesopotamia, the Akkadian civilization compiles the earliest known astronomy records.

Akkadian Tablet

350 BC

The Chinese astronomer Shi Shen creates a catalog of 800 stars.

130 BC

The Greek astronomer Hipparchus uses various tools to study the positions of stars. He creates the first accurate star map of more than 850 of the brightest stars.

Hipparchus

BC // AD

AD 150

Map Based on Ptolemy's Research

Claudius Ptolemy of Egypt names 48 constellations.

Johannes Kepler

1609

German astronomer Johannes Kepler publishes his laws about the motion of the planets. This is the first mathematical explanation that Earth revolves around the Sun.

1834

William Herschel's map of the sky defines the size and shape of the **Milky Way**, where Earth is located.

William Herschel

1922

The International Astronomical Union names 88 official constellations. Of these, 36 constellations are in the northern sky, and 52 are in the southern sky.

1990

The Hubble Space Telescope is launched.

Hubble Telescope

2018

The James Webb Space Telescope is scheduled for launch. More powerful than Hubble, it will search for galaxies not yet seen by humans.

Andromeda over Time

Astronomers have studied the Andromeda constellation for centuries. They have made many important discoveries about it. Scientists also study galaxies and other objects in space that appear in the same area of the sky as the constellation. One of these is called the Andromeda Galaxy.

AD 964 The Andromeda Galaxy

The Persian astronomer Abd al-Rahman al-Sufi first observed the Andromeda Galaxy in 964. He called it a "little cloud." The galaxy can be seen just above the constellation. Today, it is also called Messier 31, or M31. Scientists thought it was a **nebula** but know now that it is a spiral galaxy like the Milky Way. This means it has long arms curving around the galaxy's center, similar to a pinwheel. The Andromeda Galaxy is 2.3 **light-years** away from the Milky Way, which makes it the nearest neighbor of Earth's galaxy.

1749 Messier 32

The French astronomer Guillaume Le Gentil discovered what is now called Messier 32 in 1749. Scientists know now that M32 is a small elliptical galaxy, which means that it has the shape of a stretched circle. It is bright enough to be seen with a small telescope. M32 is sometimes called Le Gentil.

1872, 1885 The Andromedids

Pieces of comets can break off and become ***meteors****. Large numbers of meteors that appear together are called meteor showers. The Andromedids meteor shower seems to arise in Andromeda. The meteor shower can be seen each November. It was especially large in 1872 and 1885.*

1924 Edwin Hubble and Andromeda

Astronomer Edwin Hubble used a powerful new telescope to study the sky in the 1920s. He looked at M31, which appeared to be a nebula, and was able to prove that it was really a galaxy. This meant that the Milky Way was only one of many galaxies in the **universe**.

1940 Radio Waves from Andromeda

Grote Reber was a pioneer in a branch of science called **radio astronomy**. In 1940, he became the first person to detect the type of **electromagnetic waves** known as radio waves coming from the Andromeda Galaxy. Radio astronomy made it possible for scientists to view many objects in space that emit, or give off, radio waves.

2009 Planets in Andromeda

In 2009, astronomers in Italy found the first evidence of a planet orbiting a star in the Andromeda Galaxy. The scientists could not see the planet. They observed that rays of light were bending in an area near the star. The scientists concluded that the gravity of a planet must be bending the light toward the planet.

Mapping Planetariums

At a planetarium, visitors can see exhibits about space and images of the night sky. A large room in the planetarium, often called a sky theater, has a dome-shaped ceiling. Pictures of objects in space are shown on the ceiling, while viewers listen to information about those objects. Some planetariums have telescopes for visitors to see the night sky for themselves. This map shows where some of the best-known planetariums in the United States can be found.

Washington
Montana
Oregon
Idaho
Wyoming
Nevada
Utah
Colorado
California
Arizona
New Mexico
Pacific Ocean

Gates Planetarium, Denver, Colorado

Morrison Planetarium,
San Francisco, California

Samuel Oschin Planetarium,
Los Angeles, California
The Samuel Oschin Planetarium is part of the Griffith **Observatory**. It presents four different sky shows each day. The observatory also has a museum with exhibits on the history of astronomy and on features of the universe. Each evening, people can view the night sky for free through telescopes at the observatory.

0 250 Miles
0 250 Kilometers

Adler Planetarium,
Chicago, Illinois
Hayden Planetarium, New York, New York
Strasenburgh Planetarium,
Rochester, New York
Albert Einstein Planetarium,
Washington, D.C.
The Albert Einstein Planetarium is part of the National Air and Space Museum. The planetarium's sky theater makes visitors feel as if they are flying through space during the shows.
Morehead Planetarium, Chapel Hill, North Carolina
The Morehead Planetarium and Science Center at the University of North Carolina is the largest full-dome planetarium in the southeastern United States. Its theater offers many different shows. Visitors can also take part in live science demonstrations in the Science Stage. The planetarium has summer science camps and an after-school club for students.
Burke Baker Planetarium,
Houston, Texas
UNITED STATES
North Dakota
South Dakota
Nebraska
Kansas
Oklahoma
Texas
Minnesota
Iowa
Missouri
Arkansas
Louisiana
Wisconsin
Illinois
Michigan
Indiana
Ohio
Kentucky
Tennessee
Mississippi
Alabama
Georgia
West Virginia
Virginia
North Carolina
South Carolina
Pennsylvania
New York
Maine
Vermont
New Hampshire
Massachusetts
Rhode Island
Connecticut
New Jersey
Delaware
Maryland
Gulf of Mexico
Atlantic Ocean

Careers in Astronomy

ASTRONOMERS often study for many years to prepare for their careers. Many future astronomers take classes in mathematics, physics, and other types of science during high school. At college, they often study physics, mathematics, engineering, and computer science. After graduating, many astronomers go on to receive a master's or doctor's degree. Astronomers often spend many years doing research to try to answer questions about objects in space.

COMPUTER SCIENTISTS design computer systems and hardware for scientific equipment. They may also program computers and develop software that astronomers and other scientists need in their work. People who want to be computer scientists often study physics, math, software engineering, and programming. Computer scientists need to be organized and have good problem-solving skills.

EDUCATORS teach classes and lead educational activities about astronomy at science museums. They also create programs to inform the public about astronomy and space. People who want to become educators need a strong interest in astronomy and should be comfortable with public speaking. They should study math, science, and computers in high school and college.

Sky Facts

COLLIDING GALAXIES

The Milky Way and the Andromeda Galaxy are moving closer together. Astronomers believe that the two galaxies will collide in about 4 billion years. Eventually, the two galaxies will merge.

Snowball in SPACE

The Blue Snowball Nebula in the Andromeda constellation has at its center a faint blue star known as a white dwarf. It was once a red giant but then lost its outer shell.

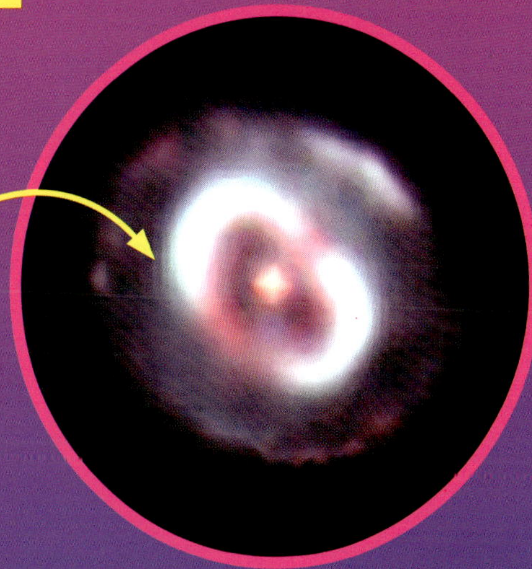

Close Neighbor

The star in the Andromeda constellation that is nearest to Earth is Ross 248. However, the star is still 10 light-years away. One light-year is almost 6 trillion miles (9.5 trillion kilometers).

Astronomy Q and A

	Question	Answer
1	**Why are some stars brighter than others?**	Not all stars are the same distance from Earth. Closer stars appear brighter. Stars also have different sizes. Bigger stars usually shine more brightly than smaller ones.
2	**What is a supernova?**	A supernova is a massive explosion that occurs when a huge star dies. The explosion sends material into space. This material then forms a large nebula. A supernova produces a huge amount of energy.
3	**What is the biggest star?**	VY Canis Majoris is the largest star that has been discovered so far. It is a red giant star located about 5,000 light-years from Earth. The Sun would fit inside VY Canis Majoris about 2,100 times.
4	**What is a red dwarf?**	A red dwarf is a type of small star that is not very bright because material in it burns very slowly. Red dwarfs last for a long time, perhaps trillions of years. They are the most common kind of star in space.
5	**What is a shooting star?**	Although it looks like a star speeding across the sky, a shooting star is not really a star at all. It is a meteor that starts to burn up when it enters Earth's atmosphere. The burning rock causes a streak of light.

Make a Flashlight Constellation

You can create your own constellation and view it without even going outside at night. Use a star map to choose a constellation. Then make your very own version of the pattern made by the stars in the sky.

What You Need:

- Small bowl
- Construction paper
- Scissors
- Star map of a constellation
- Pencil
- Toothpick
- Flashlight

1 Use the bowl and pencil to trace a circle onto the construction paper.

2 Cut out the circle using the scissors.

3 Follow the star map and use the pencil to mark the stars of the constellation on the circle.

4 Use the toothpick to punch holes through the paper where the stars are located.

5 Take the flashlight and paper into a dark room.

6 Hold up the paper in the direction of a bare wall.

7 Shine the flashlight toward the paper. You will then see the constellation appear on the wall.

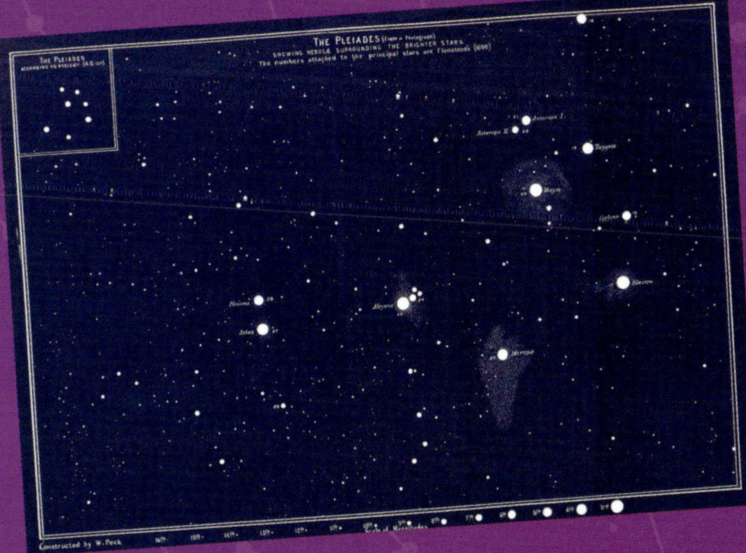

Know Your Stars Quiz

ANSWERS:
1. Alpha Andromedae, also called Alpheratz or Sirrah
2. Edwin Hubble **3.** 2009
4. Cassiopeia **5.** Los Angeles, California **6.** the Andromedids
7. Abd al-Rahman al-Sufi
8. Beta Andromedae, or Mirach
9. to know when to plant and harvest their crops **10.** Ross 248

Key Words

binary star: a system of two stars that orbit a common center of gravity, the force that pulls objects toward one another

civilizations: groups of people who live in the same area and share beliefs and a way of life

comets: large balls of ice and rock in space that travel around the Sun

electromagnetic waves: electrical and magnetic vibrations that travel through the air or through space

galaxies: groups of millions or billions of stars, as well as the dust and gas around them

gas giant: a large planet that is mostly made up of gases and not rock or other solid material

hemisphere: one half of a sphere such as Earth

light-years: distances that light travels in one year

meteors: pieces of rock traveling in space that enter Earth's atmosphere, the layer of air around the planet

Milky Way: the galaxy that includes Earth and its solar system and appears as a white band of stars in the night sky

nebula: a cloud of gas and dust in space

observatory: a building containing equipment used to observe and study stars, planets, weather, and other natural occurrences

orbit: to travel around an object in a curved path

radio astronomy: the branch of astronomy dealing with radio waves that are received from outside Earth's atmosphere

red giant: a star that is becoming bigger and cooler, has a red color, and will eventually explode

telescopes: devices used to detect and observe distant objects

universe: all of space and the objects in space

Index

LIGHTBOX

SUPPLEMENTARY RESOURCES

Click on the plus icon found in the bottom left corner of each spread to open additional teacher resources.

- Download and print the book's quizzes and activities
- Access curriculum correlations
- Explore additional web applications that enhance the Lightbox experience

LIGHTBOX DIGITAL TITLES

Packed full of integrated media

VIDEOS

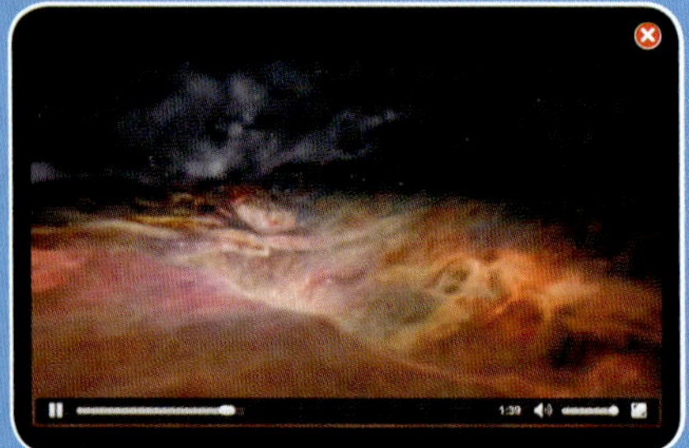

INTERACTIVE MAPS

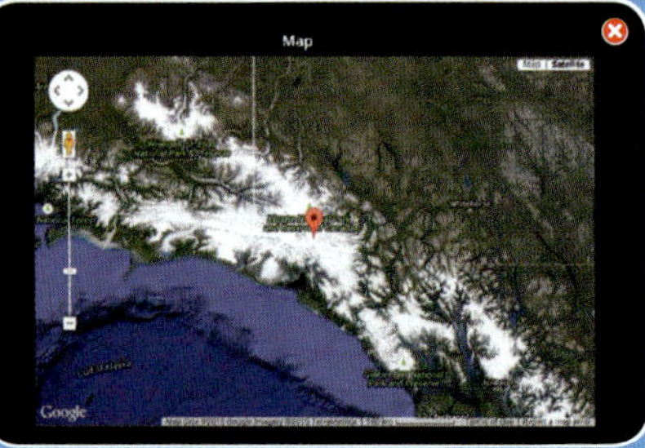

WEBLINKS

SLIDESHOWS

QUIZZES

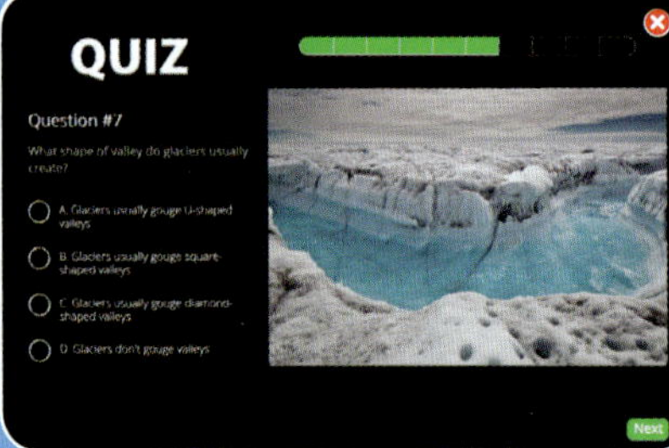

OPTIMIZED FOR

- ✓ TABLETS
- ✓ WHITEBOARDS
- ✓ COMPUTERS
- ✓ AND MUCH MORE!

Published by Smartbook Media, Inc.
350 5th Avenue, 59th Floor
New York, NY 10118
Website: www.openlightbox.com

Library of Congress Cataloging-in-Publication Data

Rose, Simon, 1961- author.
Andromeda / Simon Rose.
pages cm. -- (The Myth and Science of Astronomy)
Includes index.
ISBN 978-1-5105-0012-9 (hard cover : alk. paper) --
ISBN 978-1-5105-0265-9 (soft cover : alk. paper) --
ISBN 978-1-5105-0013-6 (multi-user ebook)
1. Constellations--Juvenile literature. 2. Constellations--Folklore--Juvenile literature. 3. Stars--Folklore--Juvenile literature. 4. Astronomy--History--Juvenile literature. 5. Andromeda, Princess, daughter of Cepheus, King of Ethiopia (Mythological character)--Juvenile literature. 6. Andromeda (Constellation)--Juvenile literature. 7. Andromeda Galaxy--Juvenile literature. I. Title.
QB802.R657 2016
523.8--dc23
2014041040

Printed in Brainerd, Minnesota, United States
1 2 3 4 5 6 7 8 9 19 18 17 16 15

052015
051115

Project Coordinator Aaron Carr
Art Director Terry Paulhus

Note: Constellations shown on pages 6 and 7 are not necessarily in their actual positions in the night sky.

Photo Credits
Every reasonable effort has been made to trace ownership and to obtain permission to reprint copyright material. The publisher would be pleased to have any errors or omissions brought to its attention so that they may be corrected in subsequent printings.

The publisher acknowledges Getty Images as its primary photo supplier for this title.